DONATED TO THE PATRONS
OF THE THOROLD LIBRARY
BY THE ILLUSTRATOR.

JENNIFFER JULICH

I hope that this 3rd book
in the series 'I CAN' empowers
children of all ages!

Jennifer Julich 2016

BE ME

"This book teaches us to celebrate our uniqueness and diversity. A must have for all children!"

DR. KEVIN LEMAN

New York Times Bestselling Author of *Have a New Kid by Friday* and *The Birth Order Book*

Miriam Laundry

pictures by Jenniffer Julich

Photography (back cover) by Terri Schous Photography
Photography (page 27) by Nicole Arnt Photography & Design
Layout by Electra Communications www.electracommunications.com
Editing by Brian Cretney

ISBN 978-0-9938964-3-9 Paperback
ISBN 978-0-9938964-2-2 Hardback
Cataloguing in Publication Data available upon request from Library and Archives Canada.

Cover Design and illustrations by Jenniffer Julich of Jnnffr Productions
www.jnnffr.com

Printed in Canada

FIRST EDITION

www.LaundryBooks.com

This book is dedicated to all who feel a little different at times.

Your difference is what makes you YOU!

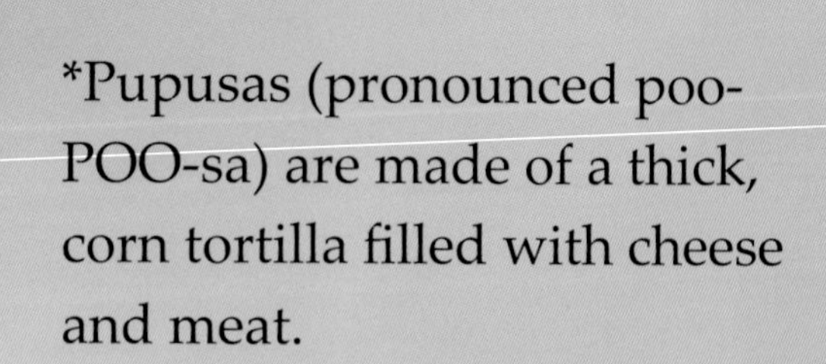

*Pupusas (pronounced poo-POO-sa) are made of a thick, corn tortilla filled with cheese and meat.

“EWW, what is *that*?” asked Alex, pointing at Maria’s food.

“It’s…um…my pupusa,” answered Maria quietly.

(poo-POO-sa)

"Did you say *poo poo*? You're eating **poo poo**?" Alex smiled at the sound of the word.

"It's pronounced *poo-POO-sa,*" said Maria, turning bright red.

"Uh...my mom must have given me my dad's lunch," she explained as she threw her lunch in the garbage.

Maria listened to her stomach gurgle as she sat quietly, wishing she fit in. *"Why do I have to be so different from everyone else?"* she worried.

Maria heard Alex again.

"Eww, what's *that*?" asked Alex, pointing at Emily's food, "and why are you eating it with sticks?"

"This is sushi. It's Japanese food. It's my favourite!" explained Emily. "And these are called chopsticks. They are fun to use. Do you want to try a piece?"

Alex nodded. He nibbled at first, then shoved the entire piece of sushi into his mouth. "Delicious!"

Maria couldn't help but notice. *"Emily is different too. Her family is from Japan and she also eats different food."*

Maria wondered why Alex's comments didn't seem to bother Emily.

The rest of the afternoon, Maria could barely focus, not even when Mrs. Ruby made her big announcement.

"Our next project is called *Discovery,*" Mrs. Ruby informed the class. "You have one week to report back what you discovered using your new magnifying glass."

Everyone was excited about the project. Everyone but Maria. She couldn't seem to think of anything except her silly pupusa.

Just then, the bell rang.

Molly noticed Maria walking all alone.
"Hey, Maria," called Molly. "I made something for you today."

Maria looked confused.
"What does that mean?"

"It's easy – always **BE YOU**," explained Molly before dashing off for home."

Maria thought about the **BE YOU** card a lot that evening.

She thought about it during dance lessons...

...at dinner...

...until she fell asleep.

The next morning during recess, Maria heard Alex talking to his brother.

"Hey Andy, put down that book and come make a snow monster with me."

But Andy didn't even look up from his book.

"Cool, check it out!" exclaimed Andy. "These snowflakes really *are* different, just like the book says."

Andy continued, "Did you know that snow is not *really* white? It actually has no color; it just *looks* white because of the sun's reflection."

"Oh, you and your books," sighed Alex, glancing over to see Maria and Molly making snow angels.

"Hey Molly, you forgot your glasses!" commented Alex.

"But I don't wear glasses," Molly replied.

"Well maybe you should," snickered Alex. "Your mittens are different colors… that's just weird."

"It's not *weird*, it's just *ME*! These are my two favorite colors."

Molly stood up tall. "Alex, why don't you be YOU and I'll be ME."

Alex just walked away.

Maria laid still in the snow, thinking about the BE YOU card some more.

"Hmm. Molly's
a little different too.

And so is Andy.

And, of course,
Alex is different.

Hey…we are
ALL *different,*
just like…"

At that very instant, Maria knew exactly what discovery she would share for Presentation Day.

After school, Maria rushed home with only one thing on her mind: her new discovery.

The next morning, Andy was picked to present first.
He talked about snowflakes.

When he was done,
Maria silently begged,
"Please pick me next. Please pick me next."

"Our next presenter for our *Discovery* project is... MARIA!" said Mrs. Ruby picking a card.

Maria stood up with a big smile and made her way to the front of the class.

"My discovery is…our *fingerprints*!" announced Maria looking over at Alex.

"Alex, can you help me?" asked Maria.

"Please put your finger in this ink pad for me," instructed Maria.

"Sure," said Alex. "But you're going to discover a lot more than just different fingerprints," joked Alex, proudly displaying his dirty nails.

Maria pressed Alex's finger on the ink pad and then pressed his finger on a piece of paper. She did the same with her finger.

"Take a look at these two fingerprints," instructed Maria, handing him the magnifying glass. "Are they similar or different?"

"Oh cool..." said Alex as he looked closely at both fingerprints. "They are VERY different!"

Then, Maria shared her *other* discovery.
"We are each like fingerprints. We are all different.
We are all special just the way we are."

Maria went and stood beside Emily.

"Emily is unique because she loves to eat sushi with her chopsticks," explained Maria with a smile.

"Andy is unique because he is super smart and loves to read," said Maria.

"...ALL THE TIME!" clarified Alex.

"Molly has her own unique fashion style," Maria said.

"As for me? I discovered that I CAN BE ME. I don't need to be like anyone else. I am happiest being ME. I am unique because my parents are from El Salvador and I love to eat pupusas – even if they have a funny name," said Maria proudly.

"Thank you, Maria," said Mrs. Ruby smiling. "You've put your 'finger' on a very important lesson!"

"Next, we have Alex!" announced Mrs. Ruby as she picked his card.

Alex went up, leaving his project behind. He was deep in thought as he held the magnifying glass over his mouth.

The class waited but he just stood there silently.

Finally, Maria asked. “You discovered your lips?”
The class laughed.

“No,” said Alex, “I, um…discovered that I have to watch my mouth. Words can hurt people.” Alex looked at Maria.

Maria stood up. “Sooo… does that mean you want to try my pupusa?”

"Sure! I'll try your poo-POO-sa," smirked Alex, pulling something from his pocket, "...as long as *you* try one of these."

Maria looked carefully. "EWW! What is *that*?" she asked.

Alex held up a bag and smiled.

"I CAN" Book Series

The "I CAN" book series empowers children to believe in themselves and their abilities.

It is this "I CAN" attitude that helps raise confident individuals. Once children understand they are responsible for their results, they are able to make changes.

The words that follow I CAN become very important. This is the reason we bring you the "I CAN" book series.

I CAN BELIEVE IN MYSELF

Book Description – Molly has been chosen to be the next Star of the Day! Most kids would be excited. Molly, however, is terrified! She just CAN'T speak in front of her class. She worries all day. She frets all night. "I CAN'T… I CAN'T…. I CAN'T," Molly convinces herself. Or can she?

"I CAN Believe in Myself" is a book that challenges children to change the way they think. Other themes in this book include compassion, confidence and self-esteem.

I CAN MAKE A DIFFERENCE

Book Description – Alex cannot believe it! He and his classmates are going to be given ten dollars each! Finally, Alex can buy that brand new basketball he's been wanting! But his fun gets fouled when he discovers that he must spend his gift to make a difference in someone else's life. To make matters even worse, Alex loses his money! How is he ever going to make a difference now?

"I CAN Make a Difference is a book that shows children how they can make a difference for others by using their time, talents or treasures.

The "I CAN" books have garnered multiple awards, including a Mom's Choice Award and a Reader's Favourite Award. The books are #1 Amazon Best Sellers, and have set a Guinness World Record™.

Invite Miriam to Speak at Your School

Miriam would love to visit your school!

Her presentations are all about empowering children with the I CAN message! In addition to school author visits, she delivers a great I CAN message for teachers on how to create an I CAN attitude in the classroom through her Teacher Workshops.

Not local? A virtual Skype Author Visit is always a great option.

You can find out more details at **www.laundrybooks.com,** OR feel free to email us **info@laundrybooks.com**

This book belongs to: